SECONDHAND SLICE

BY JAKE MADDOX

Text by Brandon Terrell
Illustrated by Aburtov

STONE ARCH BOOKS
a capstone imprint

Jake Maddox Sports Stories are published by
Stone Arch Books
a Capstone Imprint
1710 Roe Crest Drive
North Mankato, Minnesota 56003

www.mycapstone.com

Library of Congress Cataloging-in-Publication Data is available on the Library of
Congress website.

ISBN: 978-1-4965-5864-0 (library binding)
ISBN: 978-1-4965-5866-4 (paperback)
ISBN: 978-1-4965-5868-8 (eBook PDF)

Summary: Thirteen-year old Ben Malone is the son of the head groundskeeper at
the exclusive golf club, Strongwood, a course Ben has never played because they
cannot afford the fee—but when his best friend puts up the money to enter him in a
junior tournament at the club, Ben is forced to confront his own lack of confidence
(and his wicked slice).

Editor: Nate LeBoutillier
Designer: Brent Slingsby
Production Specialist: Tori Abraham

Printed in Canada.
010808S18

TABLE OF CONTENTS

CHAPTER 1
FORE!

Thirteen-year old Ben Malone groaned. He emerged from his bed like a zombie pulling itself from the grave.

"Rise and shine!" his dad said.

Ben's eyes were gritty with sleep. He looked out the bedroom window. "It's still dark outside," he croaked.

"Yep." His dad sipped coffee from his mug.

Ben sat up. He patted his shaggy brown hair back into place. "What am I getting myself into?" he asked.

His dad laughed. "You were the one who asked to go to work with me this morning, pal. So get dressed. Let's go."

Gary Malone was a new employee of Strongwood Country Club, the nicest golf course in town. Ben had never played there.

Even though his dad was the head groundskeeper, his family couldn't afford a discount membership. So Ben golfed at Valley View, a nine-hole public course.

The sky brightened as Ben climbed into his dad's rusty, dented pick-up and they drove. When they pulled up next to Strongwood's maintenance shed, Ben got out and zipped up his hoodie. The morning was chilly.

Ben's dad drove a riding lawnmower out of the shed. "Hop on, kiddo," he said. "Time to maintain the fairways and greens."

Ben jumped on and sat on a small back seat. The mower rumbled, and dew glistened off the trimmed fairway. Wet grass stuck to the side of the mower as they cruised along.

Together, Ben and his dad patched large divots in the tee boxes. They artfully raked the sand in each bunker.

When they were done, the sun was up. The morning chill had burned away. Returning to the pick-up, Ben's dad said he had a surprise.

"What is it?" Ben asked.

His dad reached into the truck bed. He drew out a navy blue golf bag. The clubs inside rattled against each other as he held it up. "Ta-da!"

"Uh, Dad," Ben said. "I hate to ruin the surprise, but those are just my clubs."

"I know," said Ben's dad. "Technically they're *my* old clubs. But I brought them along, so we could play eighteen."

"Here?" Ben looked out across the hilly golf course.

Several older golfers had begun their morning round. One older guy wore a pair of colorful plaid pants.

"Yes," his dad said. "Here."

Ben hesitated. He didn't think his crummy set of clubs would be up to the task of playing at Strongwood. "I don't know."

"Come on." His dad took out a second set of clubs. "There's a cart waiting for us."

"A cart?" Ben wasn't sure about that. He'd usually just carried his battered bag around the course. Riding in a cart seemed wrong somehow.

Ben's worries washed away the moment he stepped on the first tee box. It was a par four, 350 yards in distance. The hole was straight ahead, with a pair of bunkers on either side of the putting green.

Ben gripped his driver and swung hard. His club head struck the ball with a loud *TING!* The ball carried a bit. Then it sliced to the right side of the fairway. It landed in the rough.

"Not too shabby," his dad said.

Ben parred three of the first four holes. On the fourth, he sank a 20-foot putt. The putt broke perfectly into the cup for a birdie.

Ben's dad whooped. Two men on the fairway beside them turned their heads in alarm. One was the man in the plaid pants.

On the fifth tee box, Ben looked out at the fairway. It was a long, straight par five. Trees loomed on each side of the fairway.

Ben placed his ball on a tee and lined up the shot. He drew back and swung with all his might. The ball sailed low and straight.

For a moment, Ben's drive looked like it was going to land in the fairway. Then it began to slice.

"No," Ben whispered. "Come back."

The ball continued slicing. It was headed toward the tee box of a nearby hole. At that tee box stood a foursome of golfers.

Ben gasped.

"Fore!" he yelled.

Ben's voice echoed across the quiet golf course. He held his breath as the ball soared closer to the foursome. They turned and covered their heads.

CHAPTER 2
OFF COURSE

Ben's ball landed short of the group and skipped along over the grass. It bounced past the legs of the frightened foursome. Finally, it disappeared on the far side of the tee box. One golfer pointed at Ben.

Ben felt embarrassed. He felt more out of place than ever.

Ben's dad climbed into the cart. "Come on," he said. "Let's see how tricky your second shot will be."

Ben shook his head. "Let's just wait until they're gone," he said.

"Nonsense." His dad patted the seat beside him. "That'll just slow down play for the people behind us."

Reluctantly, Ben sat in the cart. They drove toward his ball. As they got closer, Ben saw that the foursome was made up of two men and two boys about his age.

One of the men smiled. He was tall with perfectly-combed gray hair and sharp clothes. "Hello, Gary," the man said to Ben's dad. "The course looks lovely today."

"Thank you, Mr. Lonigren," said Ben's dad. He turned to Ben. "Mr. Lonigren is the country club's golf pro. He teaches lessons."

"And this must be your son," Mr. Lonigren said.

Ben nodded. "I'm Ben. Nice to meet you."

"Nothing better than hitting the links with your old man," Mr. Lonigren said. "Isn't that right, Evan?"

One boy perked up, saying, "Yes, sir."

The boy was lean and lanky. He wore a crisp, white polo shirt. His shoes gleamed. Suddenly, Ben's own grass-stained sneakers and ripped hoodie felt uncomfortable.

The boy wasn't from Ben's school. Ben wondered if he went to the private academy. He dressed like he did.

"Looks like you have a bit of a slice," Mr. Lonigren said. "Evan, be a gentleman. Show Ben where his ball landed."

"Of course, Dad," Evan said.

Ben followed Evan to a nearby patch of thick grass.

As they walked, Evan turned to Ben. Under his breath, Evan said, "Fantastic clubs. Did you find them in the dumpster behind the clubhouse?"

Ben was too stunned to speak.

"There you are," Evan said loud enough for everyone to hear. A smile returned to his lips. "That second shot is gonna be a doozy."

Ben gripped the club tight, trying to keep it from shaking. He tried not to think about everyone watching. He quickly chopped his 3-iron at the ball, hacking out a tuft of grass.

The ball dribbled through the rough about ten yards. Ben's ears and cheeks burned with shame.

He trudged up and hacked at the ball again. This time it popped high into the air. It sliced sideways but still found the edge of the fairway, about 75 yards up.

Ben shoved the iron back into his beat-up bag. The weather and the course were beautiful. But Ben no longer felt like playing golf.

CHAPTER 3
PUTT-PUTT

The day after the debacle at Strongwood, Ben and his best friend Hugo met up at Adventure Zone. The fun-filled park had an arcade, batting cages, and even a small Ferris wheel.

Twice a week in summer, kids could play the mini-golf course for half-price. Ben and Hugo often took advantage of that deal.

The course was full of obstacles like a windmill, a loop-de-loop, and a huge roaring dragon. That dragon stared down at the boys from its perch on the 18th hole.

Hugo smacked a green golf ball with his putter. It sailed off a wooden ramp, struck the metal dragon's nose, and bounced off.

"Was your slice more embarrassing than that?" Hugo asked. He blew a raspberry.

"This kid was acting all high and mighty," Ben said. "Like . . . like . . ."

"Like he was the golf pro's kid or something?" Hugo said.

"Exactly." Ben lined up his putt. "Now watch and learn, dude," he said.

In one smooth action, like the pendulum of a clock, Ben struck the ball. It hit the ramp perfectly and was swallowed whole by the dragon's mouth.

A moment later, the ball rattled out of the end of the dragon's tail and dropped into the hole.

"That's how it's done!" Ben said. He held his putter by the head and swung it out in front of him.

"Behold!" Hugo shouted. "Sir Benjamin the Dragonslayer!" He thrust his putter.

The two boys clanged their fake swords together like knights in battle. From the corner of his eye, Ben saw two figures approaching. He assumed they were Adventure Zone employees coming to ask them to knock it off. It wouldn't have been the first time.

Ben stopped stabbing his putter around. They weren't employees, though.

"Well, if it isn't the kid with the wicked slice," Evan Lonigren said.

He and his friend stood near the metal dragon. They drank large smoothies.

"And who art thou, foul peasant?" Hugo asked, clearly still acting like a knight.

"Peasant?" Evan said. He laughed. "Look who's talking."

"Sorry again for the wild drive yesterday," Ben said. He hoped an apology would make Evan and his friend leave them alone. "It was my first time playing Strongwood."

"We could tell," said Evan. "Right, Reggie?"

Evan's friend laughed. "Totally."

"At least when you play baby golf you're less likely to hit someone," Evan said. "And your clubs are *supposed* to be secondhand."

Hugo frowned as the boys walked away.

"So those were the dudes from this morning?" Hugo asked.

Over his shoulder, Evan shouted, "Fore!"

"Yep," said Ben.

"Charming fellows," Hugo said. "Come now, Dragonslayer. Another round? Show me some more of that sweet putting action."

CHAPTER 4
THE FINE PRINT

The next day, Ben and Hugo biked to their favorite store. Replay Sports sold used sporting goods. It was part of a mini-mall. It included a barbershop and a frozen yogurt place that had just gone out of business.

They rarely searched for particular items at Replay. Ben just liked to wander the store's cluttered aisles. Hugo just liked to talk.

They found the golf equipment. Ben plucked an oversized driver out of a rack. Even with a scuff on the club's head, it still cost a pretty penny.

"Okay, so do you remember that jerk from Adventure Zone?" Hugo asked.

"I've been trying to forget him," Ben said.

"What if there was a way to teach him a lesson?" Hugo said.

Ben scrunched up his face. "Like, how?"

Hugo dug into his pocket. He brought out a folded piece of green paper. "I found this taped up by the door at Adventure Zone."

Hugo unfolded the paper. He set it on an empty shelf. "*Strongwood Country Club Junior Golf Tournament*," Ben read. Right away, he knew where Hugo was going with this. Ben shook his head. "No way."

"Come on," Hugo said. "You should enter. Show the high and mighty jerkazoid who's better at golf."

"He is," Ben said. "He is better at golf."

"Make him prove it," Hugo said.

Ben snatched the flyer off the shelf.

"There's a hundred-dollar entry fee," he said, reading the fine print.

"But a five-hundred-dollar grand prize!" Hugo said. "And a set of new golf clubs."

"I don't have a hundred bucks," said Ben.

"Just think, though," Hugo said. "You'd finally have a new set of clubs for yourself. You wouldn't have to use your dad's."

"Maybe I like using them," Ben said.

"Do you?" Hugo asked. "You seemed crazy embarrassed when Evan dissed them."

Ben looked sideways at his friend. He continued reading the flyer. *"All Strongwood members ages ten to fourteen eligible. Apply online or at the clubhouse."* He shrugged. "There you have it. Me? Not a member."

Hugo said, "Read it again, dude."

At the bottom of the flyer, in tiny print, were more instructions and rules. When he read them, Ben's stomach did a backflip.

All family of Strongwood members and employees are eligible.

"See?" Hugo placed his hands on his hips like he'd won the argument. "Members and employees. Your dad's an employee."

Ben shook his head like a wet dog trying to shed water. "Not gonna happen. Sorry."

Hugo took a deep breath. "Okay, this isn't how I pictured this talk going," he said in a tiny voice. "Sooo . . . don't be mad, but . . ."

"Oh, no," Ben muttered.

Hugo flashed a nervous smile at Ben. "I kind of filled out the online application last night. And I also paid the fee already."

"You did what?!" said Ben.

"I did it for you," said Hugo. "I thought you'd love the idea."

"But you don't have a hundred bucks," Ben argued.

"Sure I do," said Hugo. "I cashed in my paper route money."

Ben groaned.

Hugo chuckled. "You can pay me back after you win the five hundred. Deal?"

Ben looked at his friend. Asking for permission instead of forgiveness was totally a Hugo thing to do.

Ben sighed. "Fine. Deal."

"Yes!" Hugo slammed his fist on the nearest shelf. A puff of dust rose around them like a swarm of insects.

CHAPTER 5
A WET ROUND

It was cold and drizzly outside, the kind of weather that kept most golfers off courses and inside warm clubhouses. That meant it was the perfect time for Ben to play a practice round at Strongwood. Ben accompanied his dad to work.

Ben spent an hour at Strongwood walking alongside his dad, who drove a caged-in golf cart with a roller and brush attachment. The cart was used to collect balls from the driving range. It picked the balls off the grass and whisked them into a container like a street sweeper. Ben snagged any golf balls that the cart happened to miss.

As he walked along, Ben pondered. He still couldn't believe that Hugo had signed him up for the tournament, but he did understand his friend's good intentions. And he realized that Hugo was right. Ben knew he had talent. He just needed a chance.

At breakfast earlier that morning, Ben had told his parents about the tournament. He explained about Hugo covering the entry fee. His dad frowned and glanced over at his mom. Neither of them said anything.

Ben knew that his parents worried about money. They worried about bills, groceries, and all that other stuff parents stress about. But Ben's parents didn't often mention it. They tried to stay positive.

"All right, Ben," his dad said, "we're done here. You can go tee it up. But be sure to come in if the rain picks up."

"It's just a few sprinkles," Ben said. He sidestepped a puddle.

"Be safe, buddy," his dad said. "Watch for lightning."

"Okay," said Ben. "Um, hey. Do you mind if I . . . ?"

His dad turned and grabbed a handful of range balls with red stripes on them. He handed them to his son.

"Thanks," Ben said.

The light drizzle created a thin haze in the air. Ben could see only a few diehard golfers on the course as he stepped up to the first tee box.

He placed a striped ball on a tee, lined up, and swung hard. The ball soared through the air. As usual, it curved right, veering off the fairway.

Before it landed, the ball struck a tree and dropped straight down.

"Shoot!" Ben yelled. He was getting really frustrated now.

He slid his driver back into his golf bag. He shouldered the bag and began to trudge through the wet grass.

Ben's round did not improve. His drives often sliced right. His chips and pitches took large, wet divots out of the fairway. And he found himself hitting out of most of the soggy sand traps on the course.

By the time he reached the eighteenth hole, his sneakers were soaked. Only five range balls remained.

According to his dad, the 18th hole was nicknamed the Dogleg of Doom. It was the toughest hole on the course, a par five with water hazards on either side of the fairway.

About 200 yards up, the fairway took a sharp turn — a dogleg — to the right. A large sand trap hugged the side of the green, as well. Not that he could see the green from the tee box.

In order to play it safe, Ben's drive would have to be straight up the fairway.

On his second shot, he could make it around the dogleg and approach the green.

True to form, Ben's drive sliced.

PLUNK!

It was swallowed by the water hazard. He grabbed another ball and tried again. His second shot landed in the same spot.

"Only three balls left," Ben said to himself. He pulled another range ball from his bag.

SPLOOSH!

Another drive went into the drink.

SPLASH!

Then another.

If it was a tournament round, Ben would have taken a penalty stroke and a drop near the water hazard.

But this was a practice round. He thought it was better to try and figure the hole out while no one was watching.

Ben teed up his last golf ball. His drive soared high across the fairway and started to slice. For a moment, it looked like it would clear the trees and the dogleg. At the last second it dropped right into the water.

Out of golf balls, Ben's practice round was finished.

CHAPTER 6
SCRATCH GAME

Ben stepped inside the warm clubhouse. He shook himself like a wet duck. He was cold and embarrassed. He didn't deserve to golf in the tournament. Not after the way he'd just played.

The clubhouse was almost empty. An elderly couple wearing old-fashioned golf outfits sat by the window. They drank iced tea like it was a beautiful sunny day.

A Strongwood employee outfitted in a salmon-colored polo shirt and white cap sat behind the pro shop's counter. A TV above him played the Golf Channel.

The employee eyed Ben. "Can I help you?" he asked.

Ben dug the only two dollars he had out of his pocket. He placed them on the counter. "Um . . . I'll take a soda," he said.

The employee passed Ben a bottle of soda. He stared at Ben.

"Thanks," Ben said.

As he drank his soda and waited for his dad, Ben noticed a bulletin board on the wall. A familiar green flyer drew his attention. Below the green flyer was another sheet. This one was a printout of names. A title at the top read: *LIST OF PARTICIPANTS.*

Ben scanned the names. He didn't recognize many but saw Evan Lonigren's name. He also saw the name of Evan's friend, Reggie. Ben's name was there too.

A thought crossed Ben's mind. *What if I just scratch my name off the list?*

Ben bet Hugo could still get the entry fee money back. Also, Ben wouldn't have to humiliate himself.

Ben saw a cup of pencils near the stack of scorecards at the counter. With a pencil, he could easily cross out his name. But walking over to the counter and grabbing one would draw the attention of the guy who was manning the pro shop.

Instead, Ben dug in his pocket and found a used tee. He would use the tee to gouge his name from the flyer. Ben raised the tee and scratched a bit at the bottom to test it out.

Suddenly, a voice behind him said, "Checking out the competition, Ben?"

Ben's heart jumped. He spun around.

Mr. Lonigren stood there, smiling.

Strongwood Countr
GOLF TOURNAM

"Oh, uh . . . hi," said Ben. "Yeah, just taking a look."

Ben slid the tee back into his pocket. He was surprised that the golf pro remembered his name. But then again, Ben had nearly hit Mr. Lonigren with one of his ugly shots.

"You look like you just went swimming in a water hazard," Mr. Lonigren joked. "You braved the weather?"

Ben nodded.

"And how's that swing of yours?" said Mr. Lonigren. "Do you regularly slice drives?"

"Yeah, I guess," Ben said.

"Tell you what," Mr. Lonigren said. "Evan and I will be at the driving range tomorrow at noon. If you'd like some pointers for the tournament, I'd love for you to join us."

Practicing with Evan sounded like a new form of torture to Ben. But he found himself nodding. "Okay," he said. "Thanks."

Mr. Lonigren smiled. "Good. See you tomorrow, Ben."

"Yes, sir," said Ben. "See you tomorrow."

CHAPTER 7
LESSONS FROM A PRO

When Ben peeled his eyes open, sunlight blasted in through his bedroom window. For a moment, he was relaxed and refreshed. Then he remembered his exchange with Mr. Lonigren the day before.

"Crud," Ben said. He buried his face deep into his pillow.

He didn't have to go to Strongwood. He hadn't promised Mr. Lonigren. But part of him really wanted to win the Junior Tournament. A voice in his head whispered, *You can't pass up this opportunity.*

So when Hugo texted to see if he wanted to hit Replay, Ben wrote back: *Got plans.*

Really? Hugo replied. *Got a date?*

Got a golf tournament 2 win.

Yeah u do! Hugo wrote. *Hurrah Lord Dragonslayer! Save the kingdom!!!*

The bike ride out to the country club was tricky. Ben had his heavy golf bag hanging from one shoulder. He began sweating like crazy. Mr. Lonigren and Evan were at the driving range when Ben arrived.

"You made it!" Mr. Lonigren said.

"Hey, Ben," Evan said. He waved politely.

Ben said, "Hey."

For a brief moment, Ben wondered it maybe Evan wasn't truly as big a bully as he seemed. But then Mr. Lonigren stepped away to get Ben a basket of range balls, and Ben had his answer.

Evan smirked and said, "You don't really think you have a shot of winning, do you?"

There it is, Ben thought. *I just knew he couldn't resist.* He turned away from Evan without responding.

When Mr. Lonigren returned, he placed the basket of balls on the ground. He teed one up. "Let's see your swing mechanics," he said to Ben.

Ben lined up. He took a careful backswing and then swung as hard as he could. The ball took off. It rose slowly, curved right, and landed just past a sign marking 200 yards.

As if in response, Evan unleashed a beautiful drive that flew perfectly straight. It sailed well past the 200-yard marker.

Mr. Lonigren teed up another ball for Ben. "This will probably sound strange, Ben. But you're trying too hard."

"What do you mean?" said Ben.

"You're making your arms do all the work," said Mr. Lonigren. He took Ben's club and waggled his head and shoulders. "Keep a nice, loose grip. Square your body with your target. When you swing, just let the club do the work." He swung leisurely, and the ball darted off the tee.

Ben tried again, slowing down his swing this time. His shot still sliced.

"Don't overthink it," Mr. Lonigren said. He helped Ben adjust his stance. "Forget everything around you. Focus on the ball."

Sure, thought Ben. *But that's kinda hard to do with you and your son standing there watching me.* Ben took a breath and tried again. The next shot sliced, but not as badly.

"It feels weird," Ben said.

"Takes time," said Mr. Lonigren.

"Maybe it's your old club," Evan blurted out. His voice came out low and soft, but his father heard it. Mr. Lonigren frowned.

The whole time Ben practiced, Evan continued to hit ball after ball straight down the middle of the range. He was trying to intimidate Ben.

"Here's a checklist to remember," Mr. Lonigren said. "Keep your feet shoulder-width apart. Bend your knees. Grip your club loosely. And take a deep breath."

Ben followed these instructions. He uncorked a drive that stayed straight and low. The ball landed in the grass right where Ben had aimed.

"By golly, I think you're getting it," Mr. Lonigren said proudly.

CHAPTER 8
A SWING AND A WHIFF

Ben was back at the driving range the following day to hit another bucket of balls. And the day after that. And the day after that. With the tournament right around the corner, he needed to practice.

Sure, he was still getting sideways looks from many of the country club members. But if he wanted to take home the prize, Ben needed to ignore their stares.

He tried not to think about them and instead focused on what Mr. Lonigren had taught him. Ben's stance still felt strange. But his shots weren't slicing like before.

The morning of the tournament was bright and sunny.

Ben had cleaned up his tattered golf bag. And his dad had given him a cap and an old pair of golf shoes he'd pulled from the country club's lost and found. The shoes were two sizes too big for Ben. But at least they weren't his scuffed-up old sneakers.

His mom wished him luck and headed off to work. Then he and his dad left home for Strongwood. They picked up Hugo.

"It's a great day to win five hundred bucks!" Hugo said as he jumped into the truck. He clapped Ben on the shoulder. "How are you feeling, Lord Dragonslayer?"

"Nervous," said Ben.

Ben's dad needed to tend to the golf course, so they arrived early. Ben hit the practice green. Ben rolled putts to the cup. Hugo watched, giving advice and noisily chomping on a bag of chips.

"This place is killer," Hugo said between bites. It was his first time at Strongwood.

The competitors began to arrive. Ben went to the clubhouse. It filled with young golfers in expensive shirts and caps. Ben hoped that no one would recognize the cap or shoes he wore from the lost and found.

He could feel some of the kids casting him sideways looks. Ben even saw one kid backing away from him, as if he were scared to stand near Ben.

Mr. Lonigren spoke. "Thank you all for coming today," he said. "Each golfer will play in a twosome. These pairings have been made at random. Pairings are listed here." He pointed to a large board behind him. "Take a look and head out to the course. Good luck, everyone!"

The young golfers swarmed the board.

Evan's voice cut through the crowd. "You've gotta be kidding me," he said.

Ben cringed. He didn't have to check the board. He knew who he'd been paired with.

Hugo checked for him. "Looks like you and Evan Lonigren are partners," he said. Reading the look on Ben's face, Hugo whispered, "Sorry, dude."

Each foursome started at a different hole on the course. They all started at the same time in what was called a shotgun start.

Ben and Evan had somehow been positioned to start at hole one. Since their hole was closest to the clubhouse, a small crowd of onlookers had gathered around the tee box. This made Ben's already-amped worry shoot sky high. He'd never golfed in front of a crowd before.

As Ben and Evan walked to the first tee box, Ben was aware of the eyes watching him. He saw his dad standing in the shade of a tree. He gave Ben a thumbs-up.

Evan strutted onto the tee box. Then he made a show of drawing his oversized driver from his bag. It was like King Arthur pulling Excalibur from the stone.

This made Ben think of he and Hugo's Adventure Zone antics. He wished he could be back there playing mini-golf with his friend. Instead he was at Strongwood, ready to embarrass himself.

Evan's drive flew high and straight and landed in the center of the fairway. The crowd rewarded him with applause.

"Thank you." Evan grinned and swooped down to retrieve his tee.

Ben rolled his eyes as he pulled out a new golf ball. His dad had casually given him a sleeve of new golf balls earlier that morning. The small gesture made Ben feel good.

He teed up the ball. Then he ran through his checklist. It took all his willpower not to think of the people surrounding him.

Feet shoulder-width apart? Check. Knees bent? Check. Grip loose? Check. Deep breath? Check.

Ben drew back his club. Exhaling softly, he swung the club back and brought it forward . . .

. . . and missed the ball entirely!

CHAPTER 9
ROUND OF A LIFETIME

Ben could hear the crowd gasp and whisper and hold back snickers. He couldn't believe he had completely missed.

There the ball sat, gleaming in the sun. Still new, never been hit.

Great! thought Ben. *I'm already a stroke behind.* He tried to not think about Evan Lonigren's smirking face behind him.

Ben needed to get away from the crowd. Without pausing, he swung again. This time, he made contact, but the shot was poor. The ball hit the grass in front of the tee box, bounced, and rolled. It came to a stop on the right side of the fairway, only fifty or sixty yards ahead.

Ben lowered his head and rushed off the tee box. He wanted to get away from the small crowd as quickly as possible.

Ben and Evan walked side by side. At first, they were silent.

As they reached Ben's second shot, Evan stretched and sighed. He said, "You know, I think this is gonna be a fun day." He put his bag down behind Ben and watched.

Ben took out a 3-iron. His third swing landed him just shy of the green. He used a 7-iron to chip the ball onto the green. Luckily, it rolled to within four feet of the cup. He sank the putt easily. He was thankful to have survived disaster with just a one-over-par bogey.

It took a few holes, but Ben's nerves finally settled.

His drives were still leaving him with long, tough approach shots. But he noticed that Evan, despite his beautiful drives, was struggling with his short game.

On the fifth hole, Ben found himself on the fringe of the green after his third shot. Ben chipped the ball. It skittered across the green, struck the pin, and dropped. A birdie!

"Yes!" Ben shouted, pumping his fist.

"Lucky," Evan said.

On the seventh hole, a par three, Ben landed his tee shot within ten feet of the cup. His putt was on target for another birdie.

It wasn't until the back nine that Ben noticed Evan starting to lose his cool. When one of his drives sailed left and clipped the top of a towering elm tree, Evan dropped his club.

And when he needed a simple tap-in putt for birdie on hole thirteen, his ball broke left, and he missed. Evan cursed.

The two boys kept track of their own scores. Every so often, a Strongwood employee checked their scorecards and relayed the information to the clubhouse.

Ben was mentally tracking Evan's score as well. Ben knew that he was just a stroke behind Evan after seventeen holes.

Now, there was only one hole left to go: The Dogleg of Doom.

CHAPTER 10
PUTT AWAY

A small crowd waited for them at the eighteenth tee box. A few of the other golfers who had already finished were there. So was Mr. Lonigren, Ben's dad, and Hugo.

"Look at all these people," Evan said under his breath. "Better not choke, rookie."

"Dude," Hugo said as Ben drew out his driver. "You and Jerkazoid are beating the rest of the field by, like, five strokes. You've got this."

Ben wished he felt as positive as Hugo.

Ben teed off first. He lined up, casting a glance at the crowd and seeing Mr. Lonigren. He did his best to concentrate. He tried not to think about the crowd.

TING!

Ben's swing was smooth. The ball
traveled down the middle of the fairway,
avoiding both water hazards. Ben was
shocked but tried not to show it. The crowd
clapped quietly.

"Nice one, Ben," Mr. Lonigren said.

Ben beamed with pride.

Evan's drive bounced past Ben's. It rolled
to the curve of the dogleg. The applause for
Evan was louder.

"See you after your win," Hugo said to
Ben as the golfers began to walk away.

When they were out of his father's
earshot, Evan spoke. "Looks like only one of
us has a clear view of the green," he said.

Ben reached his ball and realized Evan
was right.

Though his own drive had been perfect, it had come up short. He still couldn't see the green. A straight shot from his position would wind up in the trees.

"So what if I don't hit it straight?" he whispered to himself.

Ben took a 3-wood from his bag. He ignored everything Mr. Lonigren had taught him. He gripped the club tightly and aimed left of the fairway.

"Um, what are you doing?" Evan asked. "You're aiming the wrong way, idiot."

Exactly, Ben thought. Then, with all his might, he swung.

THWACK!

Blades of grass flew into the air. Ben's ball headed for the trees on the left of the fairway. Then, like a miracle, it began to slice.

Right around the bend.

Ben couldn't see where his shot landed. He grabbed his clubs and quickly rounded the dogleg.

Even from 200 yards out, Ben could see his ball resting on the edge of the green. *I did it!* Ben thought. *It actually worked!*

Evan approached his second shot. His view of the green was clear. His swing took too much of a divot, though. His ball hooked into the bunker hugging the green. The crowd lining the cart path gasped.

"No!" said Evan. He slammed his club down into the grass so hard it stuck there. Realizing he could be penalized for poor sportsmanship, he quickly picked it up again.

When they reached the green, Ben had to decide whether to chip or putt.

His ball was forty feet from the cup, and he was facing a steep downhill break.

The decision was easy. He pulled the worn putter from his bag. He stood just off the green to watch Evan.

Evan unleashed a spray of sand as he tried to get out of the bunker. His shot made it out. But the ball landed on the edge of the sand trap, still off the green.

Ben imagined he saw steam coming from Evan's ears.

Evan recovered, though. His next shot rolled across the green and stopped close to the cup. "That's more like it," he grumbled.

He's putting for par, Ben calculated. *I'm putting for eagle. If I make this, I gain two strokes and win.*

Ben crouched down and studied the green.

It broke a bit downhill and to the left. That meant he should aim just above the right side of the cup. He lined up his shot. He exhaled slowly and tapped the ball.

The putt broke downhill, gaining speed. For a split-second, it looked like Ben had misread the green. It looked like the ball wasn't going to break. But then the ball began to curve back, moving fast. Too fast. Fast enough to shoot right past the hole.

The ball hit the back edge of the cup . . .

. . . and dropped in.

"YES!" Hugo shouted from the impressed onlookers. "Eagle! It's an eagle!"

Ben couldn't believe it. He crossed the green like he was walking on a cloud. Slowly, a smile spread across his face.

"Excuse me," he said, passing Evan.

Ben plucked the ball from the cup and tipped his cap to the crowd.

After Evan sank his par putt, the competitors all gathered in the clubhouse. Many of the golfers congratulated Ben. They offered compliments on his putt and on his gutsy second shot.

"You used your slice to your advantage," Ben's dad said. He hugged Ben. "That was very impressive."

"Thanks, Dad," Ben said.

Mr. Lonigren stood before the crowd. He announced, "The winner of the Strongwood Junior Golf Tournament is . . . Ben Malone!"

Someone passed Mr. Lonigren a trophy, which he passed to Ben along with the shiny set of golf clubs. "Congratulations, Ben," Mr. Lonigren said.

"Thank you, sir," Ben replied.

To Ben's surprise, even Evan came up and muttered a quick, "Congrats." Then he slunk away into the crowd again.

Ben studied the trophy. He weighed it in his arms. It was heavier than it looked.

Hugo came up and draped an arm over Ben's shoulder. "So, Dragonslayer," Hugo said, "how many rounds of mini-golf will that prize money buy us?"

Ben laughed and shook his head. "I'm afraid to find out," he said.

"Are you excited to use your new clubs?" said Hugo.

Ben considered the question. He thought about it for a long moment and then cast a glance at his smiling father.

His father smiled back.

"Of course," Ben said. "But I gotta tell you, Hugo. There's really nothing wrong with the ones I already have."

ABOUT THE AUTHOR

Brandon Terrell is the author of numerous children's books, including several volumes in both the Tony Hawk 900 Revolution series and the Tony Hawk Live2Skate series. He has also written several Spine Shivers titles and is the author of the Time Machine Magazine series. When not hunched over his laptop, Brandon enjoys movies and television, reading, watching and playing baseball, and spending time with his wife and two children at his home in Minnesota.

ABOUT THE ILLUSTRATOR

Aburtov works as a colorist for Marvel Comics, DC Comics, IDW Publishing, and Dark Horse Comics and as an illustrator for Stone Arch Books. He lives in Monterrey, Mexico, with his lovely wife, Alba, and his crazy children, Ilka, Mila, and Aleph.

GLOSSARY

birdie (BUR-dee)—a score on a golf hole played one stroke under par

bogey (BOH-gee)—a score on a golf hole played one stroke over par

bunker (BUNK-ur)—a shallow pit of sand or bare earth

dogleg (DOG-leg)—something that bends sharply, often at an angle of approximately 90 degrees

eagle (EE-guhl)—a score on a golf hole played two under par

hazard (HAZ-urd)—part of a golf course that provides a difficult obstacle, usually of sand or water

par (PAR)—a score on a golf hole played in the exact number of strokes expected for a golfer to get the ball in the hole

pitch (PICH)—a short shot usually made using less than a full swing

rough (RUHF)—longer grass that borders the fairway, which has shorter grass

slice (SLISSE)—a golf shot that bends to the right for a right-handed golfer, usually because it is hit somewhat incorrectly

DISCUSSION QUESTIONS

1. Ben is uncomfortable around Evan. Explain several ways this is shown in the story.

2. Ben's friend Hugo signed him up for the tournament without asking. Would you have done the same for a friend? Explain.

3. Ben has a hard time concentrating when others are watching him golf, and this affects his game. Why do you think this is?

WRITING PROMPTS

1. Design your own mini-golf course and write about what it looks like.

2. Ben works hard to correct his slice. Write about a time when you worked hard to overcome an obstacle.

3. Pretend you are a sportswriter who just witnessed Ben beating Evan on the Dogleg of Doom. Write an article for the newspaper.

MORE ABOUT SLICES

A "slice" is a type of golf shot where the ball curves in flight. For a right-handed golfer, it curves to the right. For a left-handed golfer, a slice curves left.

A slang term for a slice is a *banana ball*.

A slice occurs when the golf club strikes the ball in an open position. This is usually due to the golfer's swing path causing the face of the club to open.

To fix a slice, make sure your club is not gripped in an open position. The toe, or end, of your club should be pointing straight up.

Also, make sure your feet, hips, and shoulders are aligned with your target line. Your body, just like your club, should be square and not open.